# My Health

By

Kirsty Holmes

**CRABTREE**
PUBLISHING COMPANY
WWW.CRABTREEBOOKS.COM

**Published in Canada**
Crabtree Publishing
616 Welland Avenue
St. Catharines, ON
L2M 5V6

**Published in the United States**
Crabtree Publishing
PMB 59051
350 Fifth Ave, 59th Floor
New York, NY 10118

**Published by Crabtree Publishing Company in 2019**

All rights reserved. No part of this publication may be reproduced, stored in a retrieval system or be transmitted in any form or by any means, electronic, mechanical, photocopying, recording, or otherwise, without the prior written permission of the copyright owner.

©2018 BookLife Publishing

**Author:** Kirsty Holmes

**Editors:** Holly Duhig, Janine Deschenes

**Design:** Jasmine Pointer

**Proofreader:** Melissa Boyce

**Production coordinator and prepress technician (interior):** Margaret Amy Salter

**Prepress technician (covers):** Ken Wright

**Print coordinator:** Katherine Berti

**Photographs**
All images from Shutterstock

Printed in the U.S.A./122018/CG20181005

**Library and Archives Canada Cataloguing in Publication**

Holmes, Kirsty, author
        My health / Kirsty Holmes.

(Our values)
Includes index.
Issued in print and electronic formats.
ISBN 978-0-7787-5421-3 (hardcover).--
ISBN 978-0-7787-5444-2 (softcover).--
ISBN 978-1-4271-2216-2 (HTML)

        1. Health--Juvenile literature.  2. Health behavior--Juvenile literature.  I. Title.

RA777.H65 2018            j613            C2018-905468-9
                                          C2018-905469-7

**Library of Congress Cataloging-in-Publication Data**

Names: Holmes, Kirsty, author.
Title: My health / Kirsty Holmes.
Description: New York, New York : Crabtree Publishing Company, 2019. |
Series: Our values | Includes index.
Identifiers: LCCN 2018043782 (print) | LCCN 2018043946 (ebook) |
  ISBN 9781427122162 (Electronic) |
  ISBN 9780778754213 (hardcover) |
  ISBN 9780778754442 (paperback)
Subjects: LCSH: Health--Juvenile literature. | Health behavior--Juvenile literature.
Classification: LCC RA777 (ebook) | LCC RA777 .H65 2019 (print) |
  DDC 613--dc23
LC record available at https://lccn.loc.gov/2018043782

# Contents

**Page 4**  Let's Be Healthy!
**Page 6**  Making Healthy Choices
**Page 8**  Healthy Food
**Page 10**  We Need Water
**Page 12**  Being Active
**Page 14**  Time to Sleep
**Page 16**  What is Illness?
**Page 20**  Mental Health
**Page 22**  People Who Help Us
**Page 24**  Glossary and Index

Words that look like **this** can be found in the glossary on page 24.

# Let's Be Healthy!

Being healthy means taking care of our bodies and minds, so we can stay **fit**, well, and happy.

A person who is healthy exercises every day and eats food that is good for their body.

# Making Healthy Choices

We can eat healthy snacks.

To stay healthy, we need to make healthy choices.

Some healthy choices you can make are:

- Choosing healthy drinks
- Eating healthy foods
- Talking about how you feel
- Taking medicine when you are ill
- Being active every day

# Healthy Food

Healthy foods help our bodies grow.

We can stay healthy by choosing to eat healthy foods. A healthy **diet** has many different, colorful foods.

**How many different colors can you see in this meal?**

Try to eat healthy foods such as whole wheat bread, meat or fish, fruits, vegetables, and healthy **fats** such as nuts.

# We Need Water

Our bodies need water to stay healthy. We need to drink six to eight cups of water every day.

Sugary drinks can harm our teeth.

Sugar is added to some drinks, such as juice and soda. Added sugar is not healthy. Drinking water is the healthiest choice.

# Being Active

Soccer

Swimming

Martial Arts

Exercising keeps our bodies healthy. Children should be **active** for at least one hour a day!

There are many different ways to get moving! Which way to move is your favorite?

Playing

Dancing

Running

Yoga

Gymnastics

# Time to Sleep

We need sleep. Sleeping helps our bodies and minds rest and get ready for another day.

Most children need 10 or more hours of sleep every day!

A bedtime **routine** can help us get the sleep we need. A routine can include sleeping with a special toy or going to bed at the same time every night.

# What is Illness?

Making healthy choices can help us get better when we are ill.

Have you had a cough or cold? These are illnesses. They can make our bodies unhealthy. Most illnesses go away after a few days.

Some illnesses, like **asthma**, do not go away. People with these illnesses take medicine and make healthy choices to stay healthy.

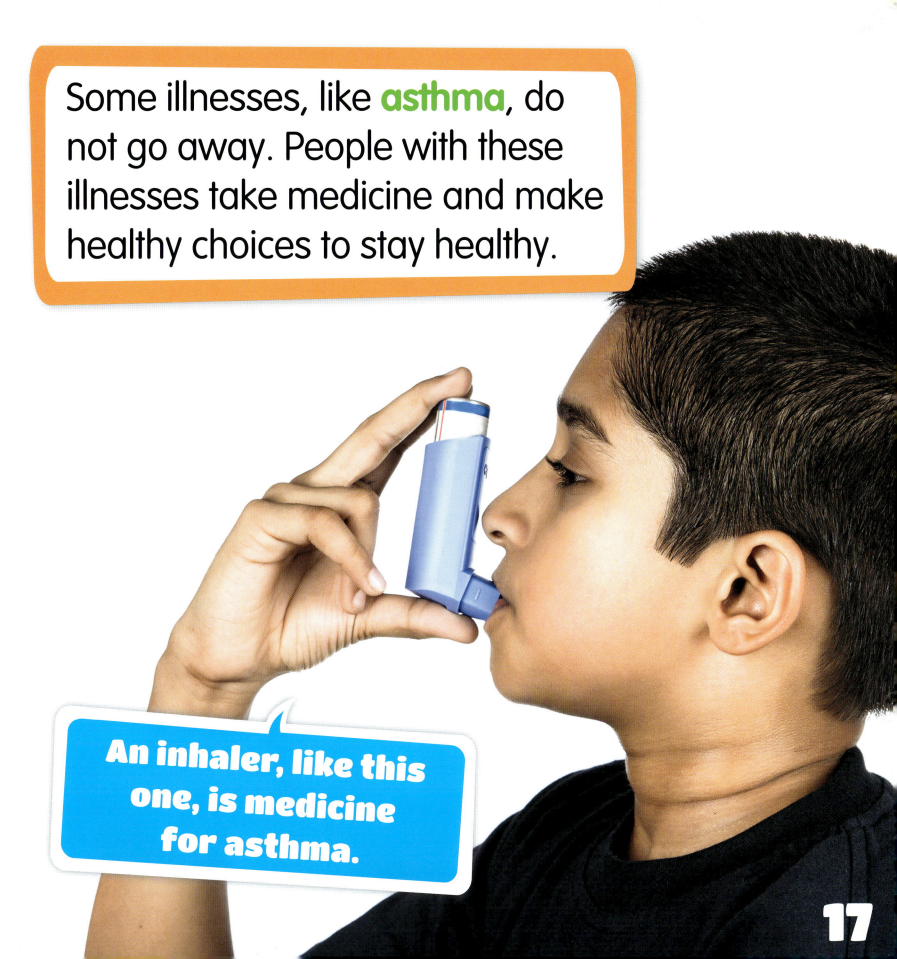

An inhaler, like this one, is medicine for asthma.

A vaccination is **medicine** that stops us from getting serious illnesses and helps to keep us healthy.

Vaccinations are sometimes called "shots."

# Mental Health

It's important to keep our minds healthy too. One way to have a healthy mind is to talk about how we feel to someone we trust.

Deep breathing can help you feel calm and relaxed.

Another way to have a healthy mind is to pause and breathe deeply when we feel upset. Try it! Take deep breaths for a few minutes. Feel and listen to them as they go in and out of your body.

# People Who Help Us

Teacher

Nurse

Dentist

There are many people who can help us stay healthy, and make healthy choices.

# Glossary

**active** — Moving in a way that makes your heart beat faster
**asthma** — An illness in your lungs that can make it harder to breathe
**diet** — The types of food that a person or animal usually eats
**fats** — A part of some foods that the body uses to store energy
**fit** — To have a healthy mind and body
**medicine** — A liquid or pill (drug) that treats or prevents an illness
**routine** — Regular actions done at certain times each day

# Index

**bodies** 4–5, 8, 10, 12, 14, 16, 21
**breathing** 21
**choices** 6–8, 11, 16–17, 22–23
**diet** 8–11
**drinks** 7, 10–11
**exercise** 5, 7, 12–13
**feelings** 7, 20–21
**illnesses** 16–19
**medicine** 7, 17–19
**routine** 15
**vaccinations** 19